MONDAYS ARE MURDER

Tanya Landman is the author of many books for children, including *Waking Merlin* and *Merlin's Apprentice*, *The World's Bellybutton* and *The Kraken Snores*, and three stories featuring the characters Flotsam and Jetsam. Of *Mondays are Murder*, the first book in her award-winning Poppy Fields series and winner of the Red House Children's Book Award, Tanya says, "I love visiting small, remote islands but I'm always slightly scared of being stranded in bad weather. Then it occurred to me that a wind-blown rock, cut off from the outside world, would be a perfect setting for a murder mystery."

Tanya is also the author of four novels for teenagers, including *Buffalo Soldier*, which won the Carnegie Medal, and *Apache*, which was shortlisted for the Carnegie Medal and the Book Trust Teenage Fiction Prize. Since 1992, Tanya has also been part of Storybox Theatre. She lives with her family in Devon.

You can find out more about Tanya Landman
and her books by visiting her website at
www.tanyalandman.com

Poppy Fields is on the case!

Mondays are Murder
Dead Funny
Dying to be Famous
The Head is Dead
The Scent of Blood
Certain Death
Poison Pen
Love Him to Death
Blood Hound
The Will to Live

Also by Tanya Landman

Waking Merlin
Merlin's Apprentice
The World's Bellybutton
The Kraken Snores

For younger readers

Flotsam and Jetsam
Flotsam and Jetsam and the Stormy Surprise
Flotsam and Jetsam and the Grooof
Mary's Penny

For older readers

Apache
The Goldsmith's Daughter
Buffalo Soldier
Hell and High Water
Beyond the Wall

MONDAYS ARE
MURDER

TANYA LANDMAN

**WALKER
BOOKS**

First published 2009 by Walker Books Ltd
87 Vauxhall Walk, London SE11 5HJ

This edition published 2013

6 8 10 9 7

Text © 2009 Tanya Landman
Cover illustration © 2013 Scott Garrett

The right of Tanya Landman to be identified as author of this
work has been asserted by her in accordance with the
Copyright, Designs and Patents Act 1988

This book has been typeset in Slimbach

Printed and bound by CPI Group (UK) Ltd, Croydon, CR0 4YY

British Library Cataloguing in Publication Data:
a catalogue record for this book is available from the British Library

ISBN 978-1-4063-4441-7

www.walker.co.uk

For Sarah and Rob
who (unlike me) enjoy climbing up things

STEVE Harris – *mountaineer, hiker, abseiler and all-round rugged guy – had just finished his training session at the local gym. Peeling off his sweaty garments, he dropped them on the floor and stepped into the shower. The water was hot, but he liked it that way – it reminded him of the steaming South American jungles he'd spent so much time exploring. He turned towards the jet of water, letting it cascade over his face and down his neck.*

Suddenly he jerked his head back so hard it cracked against the tiled wall. The water had got hotter. It was boiling. Dangerous. Frantically Steve grabbed the heat dial and twisted it. Nothing happened: the temperature didn't change. He tried to turn the water off. The control came away in his hand. He pushed the door, but it was stuck. With increasing desperation he hammered on it, yelling and screaming for help. He could feel his skin blistering, his entire body being scalded by the savage heat.

A shadowy form appeared on the other side of the glass and for a moment Steve felt a surge of relief. Someone had come to help him!

But as the face drew closer he seemed to stare into the cold, dead eyes of a ghost.

At that moment Steve Harris knew he was doomed.

DANGEROUS SPORTS

MY name is Poppy Fields. I know perfectly well that people can't rise from the dead. Zombies? Poltergeists? Phantoms? Spooks? They're all figments of someone's deranged imagination. I don't believe in ghosts.

Not in the daytime, at any rate. Not when I'm at home.

But at night, in the dark, on a remote island that's cut off from the outside world by a raging storm, when people start dropping dead left, right and centre, and you're absolutely one hundred per cent sure that no living soul could possibly be responsible for murdering them? Well, in those circumstances it's hard not to think that the invisible hand of an avenging spirit is at work. Believe me, I should know.

I was there.

It was almost the end of the summer holidays. My mum, Lili, is a landscape gardener and she runs her own firm, Green Fields and Far Away. The summer's a busy time of year for her and normally I spend the school holidays doing Not Very Much at home. But this year we had a phone call. It was a client of Mum's saying that a friend of hers was handing out free holiday places at an activity centre on the Scottish island of Murrag and would I like to go? Mum didn't ask my opinion. She leapt at the offer like she'd been electrocuted. Ten thousand volts of enthusiasm went into her answer: "Fantastic! How wonderful! Yes, she'll love it." Landscape gardeners don't earn very much, so the fact that it was free was a big plus. She thought she was giving me a treat, you see.

And why was it free? Well, it turned out that the activity centre would be opening to proper, fee-paying school parties in September, but first they needed willing kids to act as guinea pigs. It would be my job to try out everything that was on offer: rock climbing, canoeing, horse riding, hillwalking. It sounded good and, no matter how hard we looked, neither of us could see a catch. So a few days later, Mum delivered me with my shiny new coat and squeaky new walking boots to the motorway service station where my adventure holiday would begin.

The first shock we had was Bruce Dundee.

He was one of the instructors, and he was going to drive me and the other kids up to Scotland. Mum had spoken to him on the phone to arrange where we were going to meet and she'd said he sounded nice. But you can't tell how someone's going to look over the phone, can you?

Bruce's face was a mess of scars. For a second I thought it was a mask. I was half expecting him to peel it off and shout, "April fool!" Only then I realized it wasn't April.

I honestly don't think I reacted – not visibly anyway. I mean, I was shocked all right, but I didn't gasp or scream or anything. Mum, on the other hand, was a real embarrassment.

First she expelled a sharp breath. Then she tried to cover it up by gabbling at him.

"Well, this is Poppy, and she's got all her stuff. We went and bought her a new coat for the trip, I didn't think her school anorak would be quite up to the Scottish weather. It can be ever so changeable up there, can't it, even at this time of year? I've put in some good thick jumpers and socks. And new walking boots too, of course, only I do hope they don't rub – blisters can be a real pain, can't they, literally I mean, and you don't want to be caught on some hillside with blisters bursting in your boots and miles to go before you can get back into the warm. And I've put in sensible shoes for the horse riding, but no hard hat because they said they'd provide those, that's right isn't it...?"

Bruce didn't seem bothered. I suppose he was used to people going funny on him. He gave me a friendly wink and then said with a faint Australian accent, "If you're wondering about my face... It was a car accident, a few years ago. I had to have plastic surgery. Wasn't very successful, I'm afraid. Makes me look like The Joker, I know, but I'm a regular guy underneath."

"Oh, I'm sure you are." Mum turned red and attempted to calm herself. "Are you a friend of Mike and Isabella's?" she asked a little bit more normally.

"The guys who run the centre?" he replied, eyeing Mum with interest. "Why? Do you know them?"

"No," answered Mum. "Mike's a friend of a friend."

"Yeah, same here," Bruce said, sounding faintly relieved. "I've never met them before. I'm kind of a late addition, I guess. Standing in for a mate of theirs who couldn't make it. I've heard a lot about them though.

Everyone says they're real nice guys. Poppy will be in safe hands, no worries."

Mum smiled and kissed me on the cheek. Then she drove away in a screech of tyres and I was left to fend for myself.

I climbed into the minibus and said hello to the kids sitting inside. I'm interested in people. Not in a let's-have-a-good-long-chat-and-tell-each-other-all-our-problems sort of way, like Mum. What makes me curious is how they behave: what they're thinking but not saying. Studying human behaviour is a hobby of mine. So I tend not to talk very much, and keep my eyes open. You can pick up a lot that way.

Take the other kids, for example.

First there was Meera. She said a loud, "Hi, how are you?" and flashed a lovely big, confident grin at me but I could tell from the way her eyes widened that she was nervous. She was probably scared stiff about being away from home but was trying hard to cover it up.

Alice, on the other hand, only managed to whisper a faint hi before doing one of those I'm-so-shy-I'm-just-going-to-peep-at-you-from-beneath-my-fringe smiles that some girls think makes them look sweet. She wasn't shy at all: she was just acting the part. I knew right away I was going to find her annoying.

Then there was Jake: hood pulled over his head,

feet up on the seat in front of him, chev
bothering to look at anyone. He was exud
hostility but I could see right through ther.
I thought. Just like Meera. I bet he sucks his ....ib.

We sat there for a bit while Bruce did grown-up
things like checking the oil and water, and adjusting
the tyre pressure. Meera buried herself in a magazine
and chewed her lip nervously; Alice sat flicking her
hair over her shoulder so we'd all notice what a nice
shade of blonde it was; Jake blew an enormous bubble
with his gum that I hoped would pop all over his face
but sadly didn't. I wasn't sure what the hold-up was,
and nobody looked like they were about to explain
anything to me, so I just kept quiet and watched them
all.

We were supposed to set off at 9.30 a.m. but by
9.45 we were still parked on the tarmac. Bruce was
pacing up and down, tapping a number into his mobile
and saying irritably, "Are you on your way? Yeah? Well,
how long?"

"What are we waiting for?" I asked at last.

"Some kid. Don't know why we can't just go
without him. He should have been here on time,"
complained Jake.

"They're probably stuck in traffic," said Meera
reasonably.

"Who's that?" Alice pointed at a van that was pulling up alongside us.

We watched the driver climb out. She was smartly dressed in a navy-blue suit, with flat sensible shoes that clacked on the tarmac as she walked around to the passenger's side and yanked the door open. Then she started whispering fiercely to a shadowy figure in the front seat. Whoever was in there clearly wasn't keen on moving, but eventually – probably to avoid the embarrassment of having his mum picking him up like a toddler – he gave in and got out.

When he stood up I realized I knew him. Or at least I knew his name. Graham Marshall: the new boy in my class. He'd only started at my school about two weeks before the end of term because his dad had got a new job and they'd had to move house. He'd instantly been renamed Gawky Graham by the boys on account of his being terrible at sport, and Geeky Graham by the girls on account of his being good at computers and stuffed to the gills with mind-blowingly useless information.

"Sorry everyone. So sorry we're late," Graham's mother said, her teeth clenched with impatience. "We couldn't find his walking boots. You'd think he'd deliberately hidden them!"

I took a sneaky look at Graham. He was staring innocently into space and his face was giving nothing away but I thought that, if he really *had* concealed his boots, he had a devious streak that was quite surprising. There might be more to Graham beneath that nerdy exterior than met the eye... Perhaps I should watch him more closely. He glanced casually over to the minibus and for a moment his eyes met mine. In that split second I could see not only that he *had* hidden them but also that he knew I'd guessed he'd hidden them. He looked down at the ground, lips slightly pursed, and I couldn't tell if he was cross with me or trying not to laugh.

"They're all waiting for you, Graham," said his mother. "Now come on, hurry up."

Do I have to? He didn't say it aloud but the hunch of his shoulders shrieked the message loud and clear to anyone who was paying attention.

His mum wasn't. "Come on, darling," she wheedled. "You know Dad and I have got to work this week. Fresh air is exactly what you need. You've been spending far too much time on that computer of yours. A little exercise will do you the power of good. Put some colour into your cheeks."

Hate fresh air. Hate exercise. Want to stay at home. It was like watching cartoon thought bubbles pop out of his head as he stomped up the steps and into the minibus.

I smiled and said hello because it was quite nice to see someone I vaguely knew, even if he was a geek. "Nice try," I said sympathetically.

His grin came and went so quickly that if I'd blinked I'd have missed it. "It didn't work," he replied gloomily.

"You never know," I told him cheerily. "It might be fun up there."

"Fun?" he said. "Doing dangerous sports? Risking mortal injury? Outdoors? In Scotland? In August?" He sighed and then added with a sniff, "And clearly you've never heard of midges."

"Midges?" I repeated, sounding like a baffled parrot.

"Vicious biting flies. I hope you've packed an effective insect repellent. Although I gather that nothing really deters them." He lapsed into a miserable silence.

As soon as Graham was sitting down, his mother clacked back around the van and climbed into the driver's seat. With a wave she was off. At last Bruce started the minibus engine, and we headed north up the motorway to Scotland.

Scotland is a long way away. A very long way away. My bum had gone numb by the time we crossed the border and according to Bruce we still had miles to go before we reached the ferry that would take us across to the island. Meera had bought a load more magazines at the last service station we'd stopped at, and she and Alice had been ploughing through them one by one. Jake had plugged himself in to his iPod and Graham was reading his copy of *Guinness World Records*. I had a book with me too but I wasn't reading it.

I was watching Bruce.

The scars on his face meant that his expressions were really difficult to read. He didn't move his eyebrows or smile or do any of those usual things, so trying to guess his thoughts and emotions was enough to keep me busy for ages. I had to work out his mood from the way he carried his shoulders. When people are relaxed, they're all droopy, but when they get wound up their shoulders start edging up towards their ears. Then there were the little giveaway gestures – the nervous tugging of his earlobe, the little grinding movements of his teeth. I started off watching him just because I was bored, but the further north we went, the more interesting it got. It seemed to me that, the closer we drove to our destination, the more tense Bruce became. By the time we reached the ferry, his neck was as stiff as a pole and his shoulders had reached jaw level.

But then we got on the boat, and pretty soon I couldn't think about anything except how much I wanted to die.

It started well enough. We had to leave the minibus on the mainland because the ferry was too small to take vehicles. When it left the harbour, it chugged along the coastline without too much trouble. It rolled about fairly gently – enough to make your stomach feel a bit odd but nothing too serious. I suppose we were sheltered from the full force of the wind by the hills. They were purple – covered in heather, I guess – and hunched together like a group of grumpy old ladies complaining about the price of butter.

But when we rounded the headland and hit the open sea I knew I was in trouble. Suddenly it was like being on a rollercoaster. We shot down sheer wave-walls into deep valleys and then got thrown up over the next peak. We tipped to one side, the ship's railings grazing the white crests of the waves, before we were heaved over onto the other side and scraped through the frothing foam.

I had never felt so ill in my entire life. I was going to die. If the boat didn't sink, I'd expire from pure misery. I didn't much care how it happened. I just hoped it would be over quickly.

The captain was really helpful – not. "It's only a wee bit of wind you great jessies! You'll never be sailors! I don't know what they make you kids from nowadays. No stamina! Do you never eat your porridge?"

Ha ha. Very funny.

I was soaked to the skin, doused with rain and drenched with seawater, clinging to the ship's railing, which had become my very best friend in all the world. I'd ejected my breakfast ages ago, followed by last night's tea and yesterday's lunch. In fact, I was pretty sure that everything I'd eaten in the past few years had been forced out of me bit by bit, and I felt as withered and shrunken as a sun-dried tomato.

But then I saw something that sent such a chill through me that for a second I forgot how ill I was feeling.

As we got closer to Murrag, Bruce squeezed past me and went to stand at the prow of the ship. He was facing into the wind, being lashed by the rain, but he didn't seem to care. His hands were gripping the railing so tightly that his knuckles were white, and he was gazing at the shifting horizon. He looked intense – savage – like a whaler scanning the sea in search of prey. At any moment he'd reach for his harpoon.

When he turned and went back to his seat, I felt my stomach lurch with something that wasn't seasickness. His scarred mouth was wrenched into something close to a smile. But I could have sworn that, mingling with the rain and the sea spray, tears were streaming from his eyes.

THE DESERTED ISLAND

THE "adventure" part of our adventure holiday began sooner than any of us had expected. When we reached Murrag, we had to climb down a skinny little rope ladder to get to the teeny-tiny jetty. It wasn't much fun, believe me. Even though the captain's mate had tied the boat to a couple of bollards, there was a menacing gap between the side of the boat and the jetty wall that widened and narrowed with each crashing wave. If you slipped, you'd either be squished flat or end up in the water. I thought Graham was going to pass out when he saw the ladder. He was so scared he refused to move and Bruce had to carry him down in a fireman's lift. Not very dignified. He deposited

Graham on the quay like a sack of potatoes.

I went next. I was terrified too, but I was so desperate to get off that evil boat and on to solid land that I'd have jumped if I'd had to.

But seasickness is weird. Once I'd scrambled down the ladder, the land didn't feel solid at all. It went up and down and from side to side just like the ferry had. My knees gave way and I collapsed on to the stones beside Graham.

"Still think it's going to be fun?" he asked me.

"Yeah," I answered. "I'm sure it will be absolutely fabulous: the most memorable week of our entire lives."

Which turned out to be true in all sorts of ways I could never have imagined.

As soon as we'd all made the perilous journey down the ladder, the ferry steamed away, and we were abandoned in the most desolate place I'd ever seen. The wind was cutting right through me, and the rain was hurtling down. When my knees had stopped wobbling, I stood up and looked around. I was hoping to spot somewhere warm and dry in the distance but there was nothing there. No houses, no shops, no cottages, no cafes, no hotel, no church, no toilets, no bus shelter.

Nothing.

Which was a bit of a problem as far as I was concerned. "Erm… Where are we staying?" I asked, trying to keep the nervous little wobble out of my voice. I was beginning to think we'd been dumped on the wrong island. Or that part of this whole outdoor adventure thing meant we'd be living literally outdoors. Camping? In a howling gale? For a whole week? I was pretty sure it would kill me.

"The activity centre's at the other end of the island," Bruce said.

"How do we get there?" asked Meera in a high-pitched squeak.

"You're not scared of a little walk are you?" said Bruce. "It's only six miles." I thought he *might* be joking but I wasn't sure. Then he winked. "Someone will be along to pick us up in a minute, no worries."

And then a warm, wonderful sound came chugging through the wind and rain. I was so glad to hear it that my heart skipped a beat. I looked around and saw everyone else must be feeling the same way because suddenly they were all grinning like maniacs. In that lonely windswept place the sound of a car engine was bliss. Seconds later an old Land Rover came over the nearest hill and wound down the road. When it stopped in front of us I practically kissed the bonnet and Graham looked like he would weep with joy.

Out jumped a man who was handsome in a craggy sort of way. "I'm Mike," he said. "Mike Rackenford. I run the centre. Welcome to Murrag everyone. Thank you all so much for agreeing to be our guinea pigs. You're going to have a great week."

Graham gave a very unconvinced sigh but I suddenly felt quite excited. Mike was so enthusiastic he passed it on like a flu bug.

"Hop in everyone," he said, unzipping the canvas cover on the back of the Land Rover. "It's a bit rough, I'm afraid, but it's the only thing that will cope on this road."

Alice was the first to climb in, using her sharp little elbows to keep the rest of us back. Then Jake pushed ahead of Meera.

"What a lovely couple," I muttered.

Graham threw me one of his blink-and-you-miss-it grins. "A match made in heaven," he whispered as he climbed in next.

I hung back for a minute because the laces on my walking boots had come undone. I was re-tying them while Mike greeted Bruce with a Very Firm and Manly handshake.

"It's nice to meet you, Bruce. Thanks for coming. It's good of you to step in at such short notice," Mike said.

"Hey, no worries, mate." Bruce's Australian accent

sounded much stronger all of a sudden. He dropped his voice. "Glad I could help a friend of Steve's."

"Such a weird accident! I heard it was the thermostat. Is that true?" Mike asked.

"Yeah. They reckon the wiring in that shower unit was faulty. Real nasty."

My head was down and my fringe was flopping in my eyes. Through it I could just about see Mike Rackenford's expression. He was upset. But there was something else in his face too. Anxiety perhaps. Or fear.

"I'd be grateful if you didn't mention it to Isabella," he said quietly. "I mean, she knows about the accident, obviously. But I'd rather she wasn't reminded of it just now. She's been ... *distressed* ... lately."

Mike glanced around as if he was checking that none of the kids were listening. I climbed quickly into the back of the Land Rover, making sure I didn't look at him – that would be a dead giveaway. But I was fascinated. Who was Steve? And what on earth had happened to him?

The two men shut themselves in the front cab together and I couldn't hear any more of their conversation. Mike accelerated and the Land Rover shot forward, bumping along the potholed road and throwing us all over the place. We had to cling like limpets to the side so we wouldn't end up in each other's laps. It was like being on the ferry again and I soon felt too ill to wonder about the mysterious Steve.

It was a slow drive along the twiddly-twisty lane and it was made even slower by the number of suicidal sheep that lived wild on the island. When they saw the Land Rover coming they scampered happily down the hills into its path and stood there, stock still in the middle of the road, eyes blinking in their black faces. Mike edged up slowly to each and every one until we were nose-to-bumper with them. Then he hooted the horn and they leapt back, startled, as if we'd appeared miraculously out of thin air, before running away in a mad panic.

Graham couldn't stand it. When Mike hooted at an entire flock and they barged past the Land Rover, sending it rocking on its axles, he cried out.

"They're not dangerous, Graham," sneered Alice, flicking a rat's tail of wet hair across her shoulder. "They're only sheep!"

"It's a well-known fact that every year more walkers get killed by rams than by bulls," Graham told her. He knows stuff like that, you see.

"That can't be true!" scoffed Jake.

"It is," Graham said. "And it's extremely unwise to get between a ewe and her lamb. They've been known to kill sheepdogs that have done that."

I looked at their curly horns and heavy foreheads. I wouldn't fancy getting attacked by one of those. Personally, I was on Graham's side: I was going to avoid them at all costs. Little did I know that killer sheep would be the least of our problems.

Half an hour later we arrived at the activity centre. Cold. Wet. Hungry.

I was sitting nearest the door flap so I was the first to climb out and get a good look at the building. It was a massive house, all towers, turrets and slitty windows. It looked spooky sitting there on its own in the middle of nowhere – like something out of a horror film. Dracula would come swooping down off the roof at any second.

"Here we are," announced Mike. "The only house left on the entire island. It was a rural retreat originally, belonging to a rich guy who spent most of his time in the city. Impressive, isn't it?"

Impressive? I thought. Yes. Cosy? Comfy? Appealing? No. No. NO.

Heaving my rucksack over my shoulder, I walked up the steps. A young woman with jet-black hair and pale skin was standing in the doorway waiting to greet us. When she smiled I checked to see if there was blood dripping from her fangs.

"I'm Isabella," she said. "Come in, you must be

freezing. There's hot chocolate and shortbread waiting in the kitchen, and I've fired up the boiler. As
soon as you've had a snack you'll be able to get out
of your wet things and have hot showers. And when
you're ready we'll do you a proper supper. How does
that sound?"

Good, I thought. Very good. I was going to tell her
so but then I noticed that she was looking over my
head and her lips were turning a funny colour, fading
from healthy pink to a sickly pale violet.

I spun around to see what she was looking at.
Bruce was just climbing out of the Land Rover and for
a moment all you could see was his outline silhouetted
against the darkening sky.

Mike was approaching, steering the other kids ahead
of him and saying, "The kitchen's on the right. Let's
have something to eat. I'm sure you all need it."

When he reached Isabella he stopped and then hesi-
tated – as if he didn't quite know how she might react
– before putting his arm stiffly around her, and giving
her a quick peck on the cheek.

Isabella didn't say anything. She didn't even
move: just stood there like she'd been turned to stone.
Mike looked at her closely, and then said, "Are you
all right?"

Just then Bruce turned and, as he approached, the

light from the doorway lit up every gruesome detail of his scarred face. Isabella shuddered. It went right through her, from the roots of her hair to her toenails.

"What is it, darling?" Mike frowned anxiously. "Someone walk over your grave?"

Isabella gave a tight, high gasp. "I thought..." She shook her head and then cupped her ears with both hands as if she had water in them. "But that's impossible. How silly of me!" Dropping her arms down by her sides she gave a forced, bright smile. "Come on, let's feed these starving kids."

I felt pretty freaked, to be honest. Because when Isabella turned to go in I got a good look at her eyes. They were wide and staring, and as far as I could see there were only two reasons she'd have an expression like that on her face. She was either desperately upset or totally insane. Neither of which was a very comforting thought when we were going to be stuck with her on a deserted island for an entire week.

GHOST STORIES

THINGS got weirder as the evening progressed. Isabella's hands shook so much as she passed round the shortbread that the sugar on top came off in little clouds. No one else seemed to notice but then they hadn't been standing next to her when she saw Bruce like I had. Or maybe they just thought she was cold. We all were, despite what she'd said about the boiler.

We drank the hot chocolate then Isabella showed us to our rooms. There were eight of them, each containing two sets of bunk beds and a bathroom.

"When we open in September all these will be full," she said, smoothing one of the pillows. "But for now you can choose whichever one you like."

Being naturally greedy, Alice nabbed the biggest. Meera grabbed the pinkest and I chose the one nearest the stairs where I could see and hear everything that was going on. Across the corridor Jake and Graham picked rooms at the back that had a distant view of the sea.

When we'd all showered and changed into dry clothes it was supper time. I'd got over my travel sickness by then and I was starving. Mike shouted up the stairs and we thundered down to the kitchen like a herd of small elephants.

Bowls of mashed potatoes, peas, sausages and a jug of thick onion gravy were standing in the middle of a very long table. There were two benches on either side that looked like they had room for at least twenty bottoms. We sat down, but it was slightly spooky being such a small group in such a big space – we sort of rattled around and everything we said echoed back at us. It made everyone feel a bit awkward and self-conscious.

I piled up my plate with food and tucked in, but all the time I was eating I was studying the instructors.

There was Bruce, keeping himself to himself at the far end of the table. Mike was sitting next to him and it looked like he was having to work quite hard to think up things to say. Isabella was still horribly white and wasn't eating much: as far as I could see, she was just pushing her peas in circles around her plate with a fork. There were two more instructors who we hadn't met earlier: the canoeing guy Donald Shaw, who said he'd been at university with Mike and Isabella, and a younger woman called Cathy Price, who was going to teach us how to ride a horse. Donald was a cheerful, outdoors type, all ruddy cheeks and big biceps. He kept cracking bad jokes and laughed his head off when Graham asked about the statistical risks of drowning in a canoe.

Cathy, on the other hand, hardly said a word.

It was all very interesting. Isabella – who was married to Mike – didn't look at him once. If I hadn't been told she was his wife I'd never, ever have guessed it: she acted like Mike meant absolutely nothing to her. But Cathy couldn't keep her eyes off him. They kept flicking sideways every thirty seconds or so, which gave me three things to consider:

1. She fancied him;
2. She thought he was up to something; or
3. *She* was up to something and was worried that he might notice.

None of the grown-ups said anything particularly interesting so, once I'd had enough of studying them, I started to read the week's timetable, which was scrawled on a whiteboard hanging on the wall opposite me.

Tomorrow was Monday, and it looked like we would be rock climbing with Mike and Bruce in the morning and horse riding with Cathy in the afternoon.

I'd only been on a horse once before but I'd quite enjoyed it, even though I'd got a really sore bum. It would be nice to have another go. As for rock climbing... I just hoped the weather would be better by the morning. Clinging to a wet, slippery cliff-face in a high wind wasn't my idea of fun. I suspected Graham would feel the same.

Tuesday was canoeing with Donald in the morning and more riding in the afternoon. Wednesday was abseiling and then walking with Isabella and Mike. Thursday would be spent doing something called survival skills. It was then that I noticed the original instructor's name had been wiped off. It had been done quickly and the shadow of the letters remained. When I squinted I could just make out the name "Steve Harris" underneath the freshly written "Bruce Dundee". I wondered again exactly what had happened to Steve and why he wasn't here.

We finished our sausage and mash. Steamed treacle pudding with plenty of custard was next. Now, I'm not a big fan of custard – I overdosed on too many lumps once at school. I must have made some sort of face when it was put on the table because Cathy, in between looks at Mike, said, "Do you want ice cream instead?" When I nodded she said, "It's in the freezer. Over there – that big door in the corner. Help yourself."

The freezer was massive – a walk-in thing stuffed with enough food to feed us all for months. I found a tub of vanilla that was so big I could hardly lift it and scraped off a little dollop to melt over my pudding.

When the meal was over and we'd stacked our plates neatly in the dishwasher Mike announced it was time to relax. "Everyone into the sitting room," he said.

"Great," said Alice. "I could do with a bit of telly."

But when we got into the room the only thing we could see was a roaring log fire surrounded by a sofa, several comfy armchairs and a lot of squashy bean-bags. Nice enough but not exactly entertaining.

"Where's the TV?" demanded Alice, grabbing the best seat in front of the fire.

"There isn't one," replied Mike.

"What?" demanded Jake incredulously.

"The reception's so bad here it's not worth bothering with," Mike said cheerily. "And before you ask, no, you can't get a mobile signal either and we don't have a phone. We're in the middle of nowhere."

"But you've got computers, right?" asked Graham, looking as if he were about to faint.

"No," said Mike. "We do all the bookings by post and that only comes once a week on the ferry."

"But what if there's an emergency?" Meera sounded panicky.

"We can radio the police or the coastguard and they'll send a helicopter – there's no need to worry. This is an outdoor activities centre. We chose an un-inhabited island so that people could get away from it all, and I mean *all*. We're entirely dependent on our own resources here. What you need to do is rise to the challenge."

"But we're not outdoors now. It's dark," said Alice. She sounded really fed up. "What are we supposed to do?"

"We make our own entertainment."

"Such as?"

"Charades, board games, quizzes. I thought we could do some storytelling right now. Anyone care to start?"

I decided then that Mike was what my mum would call thick-skinned. The loud groan of dismay that echoed around the room, bouncing from wall to wall and back again, would have made anyone else shrivel up. But Mike just sat there grinning and looking totally untroubled. There was a long silence, broken only by the crackling flames from the log fire.

Then from the depths of an armchair Bruce, who'd been pretty quiet all evening, spoke up in his broad Aussie accent.

"I can tell one, mate. I heard it from the ferry skipper on the way over here. A ghost story. Do you lot want to hear it?"

Alice and Jake said yes immediately. Meera bit her lip but then smiled and nodded. Graham – who had plunged into an epic computer-withdrawal gloom – said absolutely nothing.

I was looking at Isabella. Her mouth had gone into a string-thin line. "I don't think we should be scaring the kids," she said. "Not on their first night."

"We're not babies," Alice replied witheringly.

So Bruce cleared his throat and started his story. He spoke in a soft, low voice, so you had to concentrate hard to catch every word. It made the atmosphere in the room really tense.

"It happened on Murrag a couple of hundred years ago, according to the skipper. In those days there were a few families farming on the island and plenty of fishermen living in a village down by the harbour. One of them was a young man by the name of Iain. His best mate, Sean, was as close to him as a brother and life was good for them both – until Iain fell in love with a farmer's daughter. Her name was Katriona and she was a real beauty. Pale skin, blue eyes and dark hair – half the men on the island wanted to marry her, but she chose Iain.

"Iain was poor, and he wanted to offer more to the woman he loved. So he decided to serve in the King's navy. They needed men to fight the war against Napoleon. Three years he'd be gone, he said, but then he'd come back for her. Katriona promised to marry him: she vowed she'd always wait, no matter how long it took for him to come home.

"For three years he toiled in the King's navy. Three years of terrible danger and hardship. Three years when each and every day the only thing he thought of was Katriona. The only face he saw when he shut his eyes at night was hers."

Bruce's voice became deeper and quieter. We all leaned forward to catch what came next.

"Three years to the day after he'd sailed away he returned with a handful of gold coins clinking in his pocket. It was a fine morning, with the sweet smell of wild thyme and heather hanging in the air. With joy in his heart, he went to the farm and called his love's name. But the house was empty.

"Then the peal of bells ringing out for a wedding was carried on the warm breeze, and so he walked towards the sound.

"Who should he see coming out of the church in his wedding finery but his best mate, Sean? And who was the smiling bride on his arm looking lovingly into Sean's face? Katriona!

"Torn with misery, Iain ran to the headland and, cursing them both, he threw himself into the sea. They never found his body. Seems there are currents around Murrag that suck you down to the depths. He's still out there somewhere, his bones picked clean by the fish.

"No headstone marks his grave. He does not rest in peace. You can still hear his ghostly cries carried on the wind as he curses the woman and the best friend who betrayed him. The story goes that one day he'll be avenged."

Bruce's voice had dropped to a whisper. For a moment there was total silence. Then the wind whistled outside like a soul in torment and the room seemed cold despite the warmth of the fire. Goosebumps prickled down my arms and I shivered.

Someone gave a small, strangled sob. I looked around and realized it was Isabella. Mike had his hand on her arm and was asking her, "Are you all right?"

She didn't answer him. Her mouth opened and closed a couple of times. Then she got up and ran out of the room. She looked absolutely terrified. There was a moment's shocked silence and then Mike followed her, closing the door firmly behind him.

"Weird!" said Alice. "What was all that about?"

"Maybe she doesn't like ghost stories," suggested Meera. "Some people don't. I'm not that keen on them myself."

Meera's unfortunate confession set the spiteful Alice off into a story of her own – a long, rambling tale involving headless horsemen and psychotic axe-wielding skeletons with red eyes. Luckily it was so dull that it had the effect of sending Meera to sleep rather than scaring her witless.

"Poppy, I didn't hear the captain telling Bruce that story on the ferry," Graham said quietly. "Did you?"

"No," I replied. "But I was pretty busy being sick most of the time. I didn't pay much attention to anything else."

"Me neither," Graham replied. "I suppose that would explain it."

We both took a quick look in Bruce's direction. There was no trace of the embarrassment or confusion everyone else had experienced when Isabella had run out. He didn't seem to have even noticed that he'd terrified her. He'd sunk back into his chair as relaxed as a well-fed cat. I decided that he must be as thick-skinned as Mike. Perhaps it was a common characteristic among outdoor types.

When Alice had finished her story, Cathy took charge. "I think that's enough for now. You all look terribly tired after your journey. How about an early night?" We leapt at the suggestion, yawning and complaining of total exhaustion as we left the lounge.

When we'd arrived, we'd claimed a room each but as we climbed the stairs the wind picked up as if the tormented soul was now screaming for revenge. I guess everyone was thinking about Bruce's story because, when we got to the top, Alice and Meera moved in with me. They didn't ask, they just dropped their bags on my bunks as if I'd invited them for a sleepover. Across the corridor I could hear Jake carting his stuff into Graham's room.

But the long day and the sea air had made everyone tired. Despite the eerie noises it wasn't long before they fell asleep.

And I was left alone in the dark to think.

CLIMBING ACCIDENT

THE wind had dropped a little by the morning. It was still gusting but at least it didn't sound quite so scarily insane.

Us kids went off for a spot of jolly rock climbing led by Mike and Bruce. Donald stayed in the centre to prepare the lunch and so did Isabella. She'd refused Mike's invitation to come along "for a bit of exercise", jerking away with visible irritation when he'd put a hand on her shoulder. But Cathy had leapt at the opportunity of going out, saying she could do with "a breath of fresh air".

I discovered straight away that Graham was right about the midges. The moment we stepped out of the door we were savaged by a grey cloud of teeny-tiny flies. They were practically microscopic but they must have had very big teeth. Within seconds everyone was scratching at angry red bites as we walked through the heather towards the cliffs.

The coastline of Murrag was jagged, as if a very large dinosaur had once taken bites out of it. Mike led us to a place where a U-shaped chunk cut through the cliffs all the way down to the broiling sea. We stood on one side, looking across to the other. The land sloped upwards over there and a section of bare, black rock rose from a narrow ledge a hundred metres above the water. "That's where we'll be climbing," Mike informed us. We all gulped nervously.

The wind was stronger here.

"At least it means no midges," Graham told me.

"No," I replied. "Now all we have to worry about is frostbite." Because, despite my super-duper-thick walking socks and specially-purchased-windproof-waterproof-all-terrain jacket, I was freezing.

Mike and Bruce started with a safety check. It took so long that my fear evaporated. I was dying for them to finish so we could get on with the actual climbing – I was sure I wouldn't feel quite so cold if only I could get moving.

Meera was peering down anxiously at the raging

sea. Jake was hopping from one foot to the other, whether from cold or excitement was hard to tell. Alice was paying extremely close attention while Mike explained about his climbing gear, but Graham was staring at the distant horizon as if he hoped a passing ship might come to his rescue. He'd informed us over breakfast that, "Climbing is number eight on the list of most dangerous sports according to the website I looked at." It wasn't exactly an encouraging statement.

"Now pay attention guys," said Mike. "As you can see, we've both checked and double-checked our equipment. You must always do that – your life depends on it. We're going to climb up then fit a top rope so it will be extra safe when you lot have your turn. During our ascent, Bruce and I will be roped together. That way if the person climbing falls, the other one is always there to stop him."

"What happens if he pulls you off with him?" asked Alice.

"Can't happen. Not with this system."

"Not even if he's heavier than you?" persisted Alice.

"No. Believe me, Alice, it's not possible. What we're going to do now is a little piece of theatre just to prove to you how safe this is. Bruce and I will go around this chasm and begin our climb on the opposite side so you can see what we're doing. We'll start at that ledge there. I'll climb a little way up, and then I'll fall – are you all right with that, Bruce?"

"I can do the drop if you like," offered Bruce.

"Really? Oh, OK." Mike turned back to us. "Bruce will fall, then. I want to prove to you how safe the gear is. If you trip or stumble – even if you fall off the rock completely – you'll always get caught. You can have absolute confidence in that so none of you needs to be the least bit scared or nervous, OK?"

Leaving us with Cathy (whose eyes were still glued to Mike), the two guys set off up the hill, skirting the edge of the U-shaped chasm until they reached the ledge.

The sea slurped below like some sort of hungry, drooling animal. It was licking into the crevices and making a horrible sucking sound with each receding wave. I couldn't stop thinking about Bruce's story. About how, if you fell in, you'd never be found. You'd stay in that icy water until your bones were picked clean by fish. It was enough to make me shudder.

Bruce started to climb. When he'd gone a little way up, Mike yelled to check we were all watching. He nodded to Bruce.

And then Bruce fell. Alice gasped, Meera let out something close to a scream and Jake whistled between his teeth. Even Graham looked interested.

Bruce dropped two metres, no more. The rope pulled tight, jerking him to a sudden halt. He swung out over the water, spinning right round in a full circle with his arms and legs outstretched before making a grab for the rock face.

But then – with no warning – he fell once more. And this time the rope didn't stop him. He plummeted into the abyss. Hit the water. Thinking it was just another stunt, Jake called, "Cool!"

But next to me Cathy gasped and I knew right away that something had gone badly wrong.

She leapt forward, leaning over the edge and holding out her hand as if she could miraculously extend her arm a hundred metres and pull him back.

We could all see Bruce floating in the clear water, face down, a cloud of blood blooming from his head. As we stood there watching in helpless horror, a wave surged in and smashed him hard against the rock. You could almost hear the crunch of bone on stone. The sea held him pressed up against the cliff for a fraction of a second before his head lolled sickeningly sideways. And then – with that awful slurping sound – it dragged Bruce out of the chasm and sucked him down beneath the waves.

For a moment no one moved. I felt dizzy with shock. Graham was shaking. Jake sniffing. Alice trembling. Meera let out a low, pitiful whimper.

Then Cathy was shouting. Screaming. Running to where Mike was standing on the ledge.

Not knowing what else to do, we ran after her.

"I have to get to him!" Mike yelled. "I can abseil down!" His face had gone a ghastly yellow and beads of sweat had broken out on his forehead. He was adjusting ropes frantically, fiddling with knots and clasps, but panic made his fingers clumsy and he kept dropping things.

"You can't!" Cathy clutched his arm, but Mike didn't seem to hear. He shrugged her off but she didn't give in.

"Mike!" Cathy took his face in both her hands, digging her nails into his cheeks to force him to look at her. "It's too late. He's already been pulled out to sea. We need to get a message to the coastguard – see if they can reach him. There's nothing more you can do."

Mike's shoulders dropped. "Right," he said. "I'll go and radio them. You look after the kids."

With that, he was ripping off his harness and sprinting down the cliff path towards the centre. Cathy swallowed hard once or twice, and with a lopsided smile that was her attempt at reassurance said, "I think we'd better gather up the gear and go back. Is everyone OK?"

We nodded, one after the other, because there wasn't anything any of us could say. We were stunned.

With shaking hands, Cathy started stuffing clips and hooks into a rucksack. Desperate to do something – anything – to help, I picked up Mike's harness and unclipped the rope. I was coiling it in the way we'd been shown when my throat tightened with shock.

The end wasn't frayed or worn like I'd expected. The rope that Bruce had been attached to hadn't snapped by accident.

It had been deliberately cut through with something sharp. A pair of scissors. Or a knife.

CUT OFF

THE coastguard couldn't search for Bruce. A severe weather warning had been issued – a big storm was on its way. No helicopter was safe to fly; no boat was safe to sail. So the police couldn't make their way across from the mainland to investigate. We were cut off from outside help: stuck miles from anywhere in a gothic mansion with a murderer on the loose.

I didn't say a word about the rope. Not there on the cliffs. I just coiled it and stuffed it in the rucksack with the rest of the gear. Because I thought that whoever had cut it would probably do something nasty to me if they thought I knew. So I kept my head down and my mouth shut, and pretended I hadn't noticed. But when

I got a chance to talk to Graham alone, I grabbed it.

The grown-ups were busy. Mike and Cathy were in the office dealing with the emergency. Isabella had apparently gone to lie down. Donald was cooking lunch. The kids were confined to the sitting room and everyone seemed too upset to talk. I announced I needed the toilet and disappeared out through the door with the smallest of glances in Graham's direction. He took the hint.

Two minutes later, I met him on the first floor landing.

"It looks like my information was correct," he said. "I did warn everyone that climbing is a dangerous sport."

"Especially when your rope gets cut," I replied.

"No!" he exclaimed. "Poppy, are you sure? Couldn't it have worn through?"

"No," I said. It was the only thing I was sure about. "There was no sign of fraying. The knot didn't work loose. Nothing gave way. It was a clean cut."

Graham gawped silently for a few seconds, taking in the implications of what I'd said. "Are you suggesting Bruce was murdered?" he asked slowly.

I nodded.

"But who could have done that?" There was a slight tremble in his voice.

My mind had been whirring frantically since it happened but the trouble was that the more I thought the more confused I got. "I don't know," I said. "Let's go through the possibilities. I suppose Isabella might have. She was very upset."

"But when?" asked Graham. "She was in the house."

"She could have done it last night."

"Possibly," he conceded.

"Or maybe Donald cut it this morning before we left? Or Cathy, while we were on the cliffs?"

"Sounds plausible," agreed Graham.

"Hang on, though," I said, contradicting myself. "Bruce and Mike checked and double-checked all their gear on the cliffs. We watched them do it, didn't we?"

"We did," said Graham. "And it was fine at that point."

"So Bruce's rope must have been cut after that. Do you reckon it could have been done when they walked round to the start of the climb?"

"That would mean Mike did it," said Graham. "But why?"

"No idea. Bruce scared Isabella with that story last night though, didn't he? Mike's her husband. Could it be something to do with that?"

"Maybe... But would that really be a good enough reason to kill someone?" puzzled Graham.

"I don't know. There's something weird going on

with Mike and Isabella. They don't exactly look happy together, do they?"

"There does appear to be a certain degree of coolness between them, yes," Graham replied.

"OK… Well, I suppose it must have been Mike." I thought for a while and then sighed. "No, that wouldn't work. The rope held Bruce when he dropped the first time. When he did the demonstration fall he was OK."

Graham recapped. "It couldn't have been done last night or this morning before we left because it was fine in the safety checks. It couldn't have been done during the demonstration because the rope held for the first fall. It leaves only one option: Mike must have cut the rope when Bruce was dangling."

"No." I shook my head, sighing. "That's not right either. I was watching Mike. His hands were full. He was hanging on to the rope when Bruce fell. Mike couldn't possibly have whipped out a knife and sliced through it, I'd have seen him!"

Graham didn't say anything so I continued. "It can't have been Mike in any case. He was so shocked by Bruce's fall. He was at least as bad as the rest of us: he looked awful. He couldn't fake a reaction like that, could he?"

"Not unless he's an exceptionally good actor," said Graham.

We went round and round in circles and finally decided that it was impossible. Nobody could have done it. The rope just couldn't have been deliberately cut without us seeing.

And yet Bruce was dead.

Donald had cooked a thick comforting soup with crusty home-made bread still warm from the oven and spread with melting butter. He laid it out on the table, and then slipped away to wake up Isabella. Cathy and Mike were still in the office, so us kids were alone again and the food made everyone more talkative.

In between mouthfuls of soup, Meera fretted. "I know it's selfish but I keep thinking it could have been me. Well, I suppose it could have been any of us, couldn't it, dying like that? You'd think they'd have checked the gear a bit more thoroughly."

Jake said, "You can't stop every accident from happening. You do stuff like climbing, you take a risk. That's part of the excitement."

"I don't call being killed exciting," sniffed Alice. "It was horrible! They should be more careful. I don't see how they'll be able to open up this place now. No one will send their kids here if they can't keep them safe. My mum will be furious when she finds out."

"I always said fresh air was dangerous," chipped

in Graham. "People are forever dropping dead when they're exercising. More people die out jogging than in plane crashes."

"I suppose you prefer cuddly toys?" said Alice sarcastically. "I can just see you playing with a bunch of teddy bears." That girl really did have a nasty streak.

"At least teddy bears can't kill you," Graham replied calmly.

Just then the grown-ups came in.

Mike was hideously pale beneath his healthy tan. Cathy was looking pretty shaky too but Donald was being kind of loud and cheery in an effort to convince us that everything was going to be fine.

Isabella, on the other hand, seemed strangely calm. If I'd had to choose the most likely murderer, it would have been her, no question. I watched her carefully. Her thick black hair hung down like a pair of curtains while she sat dismembering a piece of bread with her long, thin fingers, picking it into smaller and smaller fragments until it was no more than a pile of crumbs. Her soup cooled in the bowl without her taking a single mouthful. And when lunch was over, and the instructors began talking over plans for the afternoon, she left the table, stalking from the room without a word.

Definitely suspicious, I thought.

*   *   *

By early afternoon the weather had closed in, and the house was being lashed with squalls of wind and heavy rain. Outdoor pursuits – even for the most rugged – didn't look at all appealing. But the grown-ups wanted to keep us Busy and Occupied and Fruitfully Employed in Healthy Activity.

"This afternoon I'll be giving you all a riding lesson," announced Cathy. "The indoor school will be dry, at least, and if you learn a few basics today, maybe tomorrow we can go out for a hack."

"Do you need a hand getting the horses ready?" asked Mike.

"Thanks – that would be great." She smiled at him in a way that made me think, Yes, she definitely fancies him. I wonder if Isabella has noticed?

"There are hard hats in the cupboard over there, kids," said Cathy, pointing. "Find yourself one that fits, and then come out. We'll be just across the yard."

Muttering about the dangers posed by large hairy animals, Graham reluctantly found a hat. When we were all ready we went over to the stables. But despite Graham's warning that riding was absolutely the number one most lethal sport in Britain ("more people get killed riding horses than driving racing cars"), the afternoon was fun. We rode round the indoor school – a sand-floored barn about the size of a tennis court – on a set of shaggy ponies, who followed each other nose to tail. Cathy kept calling, "Heels down, shoulders back, elbows in!" We learned to walk and then to trot, which was surprisingly difficult until I got the hang of it. Finally, with sore bottoms and aching thighs, we went back to the house for tea, board games and another early night.

Meera and Alice were just settling themselves into bed when I realized I'd left my book in the sitting room. Pulling on my dressing gown, I went back down to retrieve it.

As I reached the bottom of the stairs I heard adult voices coming from the office. In bare feet, I made no sound, so they didn't hear me approaching. When I caught what they were saying, it stopped me in my tracks.

"I just don't understand it!" It was Mike. "How could it have happened? I guess it was sheer bad luck—"

"Bad luck?!" Isabella exclaimed, her voice tight and high as if she was fighting hysteria. "Don't you see? First Steve dies, now Bruce. It's not bad luck. We're cursed!"

"No." Mike's tone was patient, as if they'd had this conversation several times before. "It was an accident!"

"Like what happened in South America was an

accident?" Isabella's tone was suddenly so venomous that it made me wince.

"That was different," said Mike. "We've been over and over this, Isabella. Richard was dead. I had no choice!"

"Didn't you? I don't think I believe that any more. You did the wrong thing. *I* did the wrong thing. And we're being punished for it. I should never have married you!"

There was the sound of a chair being pushed back hard as if Mike had leapt to his feet. I thought he was about to yell at her but then I heard him taking deep, ragged breaths to steady himself. When he spoke again it was slowly and with extreme care as if he was barely controlling his temper. "I'm sorry you feel like that, Isabella." He gave a pained sigh. "But you can't really believe we're at the mercy of some sort of ghost?"

"Can't I? I don't see any other explanation."

"But that's insane!" he cried. "There's no such thing as ghosts! It's just not possible! And even if it was true – why kill Bruce? He wasn't in South America. We've never even met him before."

"No ... poor Bruce," Isabella said quietly. Then her voice became harsh. "You were the one who planned to fall on that demonstration, weren't you? It should have been you who died, not Bruce. He should never have swapped places with you." Isabella began to cry in soft, despairing sobs.

"I'll get you something to drink. A cup of tea will help." Mike's words might have been soothing but his tone wasn't. He sounded half strangled, as though he was forcing the words out between gritted teeth, and I realized he was extremely angry. Murderous, even.

I could hear him moving quickly towards the door so I fled upstairs, leaving my book abandoned in the sitting room. I wrapped myself up in my duvet but it was a long time before I could stop shivering.

FROSTBITE

WE woke up the next morning to find that the rain had stopped, although the wind was so strong that helicopter and boat travel was still impossible. No rescue teams would be able to leave the mainland. We were stuck here for at least another day. Once we were dressed, we trooped down to the kitchen, where Donald was cooking a big fry-up.

"Just the thing for keeping out the cold," he told us heartily. "You're going to need it today."

"What are we doing this morning?" asked Jake, tucking into a slice of bacon.

"We were supposed to be canoeing, but the weather's a wee bit rough for that," replied Donald, squinting out of the window. "There's a loch in the hills where I wanted to take you but it will be too dangerous up there for beginners just now."

"How about bringing your ride forward to this morning, Cathy?" suggested Mike. "You could go down past the woodshed and along the valley – the wind won't be so bad there."

"That's true," agreed Cathy. "Yeah, we'll do that. All OK for a ride then, guys?"

A mostly enthusiastic series of replies rang around the kitchen, almost but not quite drowning out Graham's, "Statistically speaking, more people die while out hacking than they do showjumping."

When we'd finished breakfast, it was on with the hard hats and sensible shoes, and off to the stables.

Mike and Isabella joined us there. "We decided we could both do with some air," Mike said, although Isabella's face was an impenetrable, expressionless mask. She didn't look as if she was capable of deciding anything. "Donald's staying behind to do the lunch," he added.

Cathy smiled at Mike, though she seemed less pleased at the sight of Isabella.

We were ready to go when Cathy suddenly patted her pockets. "Oh! I've forgotten my gloves!" she said. "Won't be a minute." She disappeared into the house for a few moments but was soon back, fully equipped for the great outdoors. She sprang into the saddle with practised ease, and I couldn't help feeling a little bit envious as I clambered awkwardly onto the back of the pony I was riding. I took up the reins the way we'd learnt yesterday and, nose to tail, we set off across the yard. Donald was silhouetted in the kitchen window, his hand raised in a farewell salute, as we rode away.

We followed the winding road down to the bottom of the hill, where a stone building stood in a clump of trees. Opposite it was a gate that led to the open moor. Cathy opened it from the back of her horse in a skilled manoeuvre and then led us along the valley floor.

It seemed that horses didn't like foul weather any more than Graham did. They plodded along in a dreary, weary walk, and when a sudden squall doused us with icy rain, the creatures all swung round, bums into the wind, heads down, refusing to budge. All we could do was sit there until it had blown over.

But even though the horses were stubborn and the wind was cold and the rain was wet, it felt good to be out of doors. The scenery was amazing and out here in the daylight I just couldn't believe the vengeful-ghost theory. OK, so I couldn't come up with an explanation but that was because I didn't know all the facts. After what Isabella had said last night, I knew that

Steve had actually died in that weird shower-related accident. And Richard – whoever he was – had been killed in South America. Yet another dead person. Bruce brought it to a grand total of three corpses. How were they linked? And how was I going to find out?

After an hour or so we headed for home and the animals sped up into a nice brisk walk. As soon as we entered the yard, Cathy jumped down from her horse and handed the reins to Mike.

"Sorry," she said, running for the house. "Desperate for the loo, I'll be back in a second."

By the time she'd returned and we'd shut the horses up in their stables we were all looking forward to another of Donald's hearty meals.

"Go on in, kids," urged Mike. "Give Donald a hand laying the table. Tell him it's time to get the food on to plates."

But the kitchen was empty and dark, and no pans were simmering on the stove.

"What the...?" said an irate Alice.

"I'm starving!" complained Jake. "I thought Donald was supposed to be cooking."

"Something's wrong," whispered Graham, looking at me. "He ought to be here. Something bad has happened, hasn't it?"

I didn't answer because at that moment the

grown-ups came in, and although they seemed worried Mike tried to hide his concern. "He was always doing things like this at university. He's probably gone for a walk and forgotten the time." He smiled at Isabella. "Remember when he invited us all over for a meal and we ended up having to cook it ourselves because he'd gone off in his canoe?"

Isabella didn't smile back. She didn't look upset. She didn't even look worried. She looked … what?

All of a sudden I remembered an old film I'd watched once about Mary, Queen of Scots. Isabella looked exactly the way the queen had looked right before her head was chopped off. Resigned. Like there was no escaping what was about to happen. Like she'd accepted her fate and just wanted it all to be over.

"The children need feeding," Isabella said, and her voice was calm but oddly flat and emotionless. A dead voice. It turned my stomach inside out.

"It's too late to start cooking anything complicated," answered Cathy. "Have we got any burgers, or chicken nuggets, or anything? I'll knock us up something quick." She crossed the kitchen to the walk-in freezer, unfastened the lock and pulled open the door.

A second of silence. Cathy's scream. And then Donald, stiff as a giant fish finger, fell out and hit the floor.

He was frozen solid.

* * *

It was another accident, according to Mike. "He must have gone in to get something to cook for lunch and the door blew shut behind him. Yes ... that's it. That's what happened. It's the problem with old houses – they're so draughty."

But all the time he was babbling, Isabella was shaking her head. "We're being punished," she said suddenly. "Can't you see? We should never have left him."

"Donald was thirty-two, Isabella," snapped Cathy, "the same as you. Surely he was old enough to be left on his own?"

"I wasn't talking about Donald." Isabella fixed her with a stare and Cathy turned away, flustered and uncomfortable.

"We still need to get everyone fed," Cathy muttered.

In the end she found bread and cheese and some fruit and we ate in the sitting room. They'd had to stuff poor Donald back in the freezer to keep his body frozen so no one felt like eating in the kitchen.

"It's horrible!" Meera was crying. "Isn't there anywhere else they could put him?"

"There's no undertaker here," I said. "I suppose he'll have to be buried on the mainland. But with no ferries crossing..."

"Bodies start to smell after a couple of days," Graham said helpfully. "And they leak body fluids. It's the decomposition, you see? That's why they invented morgues. You have to keep the body cold—"

"Shut up, Graham," said Jake. "You're putting me off my food."

Mike went off to radio the police on the mainland. He came back a few minutes later looking even more white-faced and anxious. It seemed the radio had suffered some sort of mysterious breakdown. He couldn't call anyone.

The weird thing was that everyone just accepted his explanation that it was a series of unfortunate accidents. No one even mentioned the word "murder" but I knew it couldn't be anything else.

I mean, I'd helped myself to ice cream from that freezer on the first night and I knew perfectly well there was a handle on the *inside* of the door. Even if it *had* blown shut, Donald could have let himself out, no problem. But when Cathy had gone looking for burgers she'd had to unfasten the lock on the *outside*. Which meant someone had shoved Donald in and then locked the door. And now I wouldn't mind betting all my pocket money that someone had also broken the radio so we couldn't make contact with the outside world.

Someone. But who? How? When?

It couldn't have been any of us kids because we'd been together all morning. Could Isabella or Mike have done it before they left the house? Or Cathy when she'd gone to fetch her gloves?

It was impossible! Donald had been in the kitchen. I'd seen him with my own two eyes. He'd been alive when we left.

It was like an invisible killer was stalking the island. Goosebumps prickled along my arms and my teeth started clacking together.

"Scared?" asked Alice cattily.

"No. I'm just cold."

"Me too," agreed Meera. "I wish we could go home!"

I didn't answer. I was too busy getting a grip. There's no such thing as ghosts, I told myself firmly. And even if there were, they absolutely positively definitely couldn't do things like cutting ropes and breaking radios and locking big burly men inside freezers. Someone was doing it all. Someone in the centre. One of them. Or one of us.

And whoever it was might already have planned another murder.

CHAMPAGNE AND ROSES

BY the next morning us kids were moving around together like a flock of anxious sheep. We ate our breakfast in the sitting room, not wanting to hang around in the kitchen knowing a corpse was in the freezer.

All the time I was chewing my cereal I was watching the others, wondering if one of them might be the killer. It seemed unlikely. None of us had known the victims before we'd arrived. We were all there because our parents had been friends with their friends. I looked over the top of my bowl and saw that pretty much everyone's faces wore the same expression: extreme nervousness. The only exception was Graham, whose face was creased with the signs of Deep Thought.

I considered Graham as a possible suspect. OK, so he hadn't wanted to come. He hated the outdoors. Maybe he even hated it enough to bump off the instructors and cut the holiday short. But I was absolutely one hundred per cent certain that he wouldn't have sabotaged the radio to the outside world. He wanted to go home: he wouldn't do anything that would prevent us leaving. I reckoned Graham's brow was furrowed because he was trying to work things out, the same as me. Every so often his eyes darted in my direction as if he wanted to talk. I was going to have to catch him alone again as soon as possible.

When Mike came in he looked like he'd aged ten years overnight. He had huge bags under his eyes and his skin had gone sort of grey and ill-looking. It wasn't surprising. Hadn't he been at university with Donald? They must have been old friends. Like Steve, I thought suddenly. Maybe even the mysterious Richard. Whatever was going on now might have its roots in the past. If only I could do some digging around!

"Look kids, I'm really sorry this week's turning out to be such a disaster. You must be desperate to get away." Mike raked a hand through his uncombed hair. "The storm's bound to blow itself out in the next couple of days. I'll get you away on the first ferry, I promise you, even if I have to swim to the mainland to fetch it. But we've a bit of waiting to do until then. We can't do abseiling but how about a walk this morning, eh? It should cheer us up a bit. The view from the top of the mountain is spectacular."

As one we all turned our eyes to Graham. "Walking," he told us, "is a relatively safe activity. It can cause heart attacks in the elderly and the morbidly obese but as none of us fits that description we should be fine."

Our little flock moved off upstairs to zip ourselves into waterproofs and lace up our walking boots.

Half an hour later we were marching purposefully towards the craggy mountain on the skyline.

It was good to be outdoors. No one could sneak up on us out here, plus I could keep an eye on everyone's movements. I was desperate for a private conversation with Graham but, even though he fell into step beside me, it proved impossible. Jake, Meera and Alice had accepted Mike's assurances that the two deaths were unlucky accidents but they were still nervous and unhappy enough to walk in a tight group that we couldn't shake off. Graham and I sped up. So did they. We slowed down. They did the same. There was no escape.

It took two hours of hard walking but at last we reached the peak, breathless and tired but kind of pleased with ourselves.

Mike was right – the view was stunning. It was all sky and water, and the land in between seemed really small and unimportant. If I turned a full circle I could see the entire island. Below me – smaller than a matchbox – was the centre. From up here I could see how remote it was. The mainland was just a grey line on the horizon.

Mike was trying with all his might to be positive but he was finding it hard going until Cathy waded in to support him with a relentless burst of cheeriness. It was like being in *The Sound of Music*. I half expected her to pull out a guitar and start singing as she pointed out areas of outstanding beauty with energetic zeal.

Isabella, on the other hand, stood apart, lost in thought, not talking to anyone. She had started the walk tight-lipped and pale, and by the time we'd ascended the peak her face had taken on a dark, gloomy aspect. I could almost see a black cloud hanging over her. Cathy's determined optimism was driving her to distraction. Clapping her hands to her head, Isabella spat, "Will. You. Shut. Up!"

Mike and Cathy looked at her aghast, but didn't answer.

"Can't you see what's happening?" Isabella sobbed. She took a deep breath to steady herself and then said more calmly, "I can't stand any more of this waiting. I'll go back now. Perhaps I'll do something about lunch."

"But we should stick together," protested Mike.

"Why?" she said bitterly. "You two seem to have everything under control. And you said yourself that they were accidents. Look around you, Mike. There's no one but us on the island. And you don't believe in ghosts, do you? What could possibly happen to me? I'll be perfectly safe." Isabella walked away without another word. I was reminded of that old film again: Mary, Queen of Scots, walking with dignity towards her executioner.

She was lying peacefully on her bed when we found her later. An opened bottle of champagne was standing on the dressing table, beside a half-drained glass.

And rose petals were scattered across her corpse like confetti.

TALKING TO GRAHAM

MIKE told us it was suicide: that she must have put poison in her champagne. I don't know whether he was trying to convince us or himself, but he wasn't doing a very good job of it. Even Meera had gone all slitty-eyed with doubt. Not that anyone said anything to contradict him. He told us that she'd been suffering from depression; she'd been very unhappy; things hadn't been going well between them. With tears streaming down his cheeks, he said he should have done more about it. Insisted she see a doctor; had treatment; it was all his fault; he was to blame.

He explained it very thoroughly and we sat there nodding as if we believed him because the alternative was just too scary to talk about.

We'd been together. We'd followed Isabella home. All the way back we could see her marching along a few hundred metres ahead of us. We'd watched her going in through the front door. The centre had been in sight the whole time. No one else had gone in or come out – we would have noticed.

I didn't believe Isabella had killed herself. And yet none of us could have killed her. It didn't make sense!

Very carefully I ran over exactly what had happened. We'd got back from the walk about ten minutes after Isabella. Mike had bolted the door behind us. He said it was to stop it blowing open in the wind but the fearful look in his eyes told a different story.

We'd gone into the kitchen in our little huddle and as soon as we saw that Isabella wasn't there we'd started searching for her. We'd moved methodically from room to room, clumping together as if a sheepdog was at our heels. Once we'd searched the ground floor, we went upstairs, checking the girls' and boys' bedrooms before climbing the steps to the top floor where the instructors slept. The door immediately in front of us had been wide open, and we'd all seen her lying there, eyes shut, black hair spread across the pillow like something out of a Victorian oil painting.

I was absolutely positive that an intruder couldn't have slipped past us.

But there was Isabella. Dead. Sobbing quietly, Mike had wrapped her in the duvet and gently lain her in the freezer beside Donald. If anyone else died, we'd be completely out of storage space.

While Mike and Cathy went to the office the rest of us crashed out in the sitting room. Most of the kids seemed bent on blotting out all forms of conscious thought: Jake plugged himself in to his iPod and turned the volume up so loud I could hear the tinny tune from the other side of the room, Meera got deeply engrossed with her Game Boy and Alice started playing something long and complicated on her mobile phone.

Which left me and Graham in one corner, whispering to each other.

"So… Do you believe it was a series of unfortunate events?" I asked him.

"The likelihood of it being a coincidence for so many deaths to have occurred in such a short space of time is practically zero," he said firmly.

"OK," I said. "Let's consider the options. The way I see it, one of the grown-ups has to be behind it all. Cathy. Or Mike."

"Not necessarily, Poppy," said Graham. "I think we

should look at everyone as a potential suspect. Including ourselves."

"I've ruled you out," I said. "I know you don't want to stay here so you'd have a motive for bumping the instructors off. But you wouldn't have damaged the radio so you couldn't escape."

"True," said Graham. "And I've ruled you out too. I reasoned that if you'd committed the first murder you wouldn't have drawn my attention to the cut rope."

"So we're both off the hook?"

"I believe so."

"Right," I said. "Well, that gives us somewhere to start. What do you think about Meera? She's been nervous from the beginning. I thought she was just scared about being away from home but there could be more to it."

We both glanced over at her. "She doesn't look much like a devious killer, but then appearances can be deceptive," said Graham.

"So we should keep her on the list?"

"Yes. But fairly low down, I think."

"What about Jake? He's so loud and pushy but I reckon he's been scared from the beginning too," I said.

"I think his apparent confidence is a disguise to conceal a deep insecurity," opined Graham. "He sucks his thumb in his sleep. I've seen him."

"Does he? I thought he might." I was pleased to have my suspicion confirmed. "So he's on the list as well. But low down?"

Graham nodded.

"As for Alice," I considered aloud, "she's got a really mean streak."

"I agree," said Graham. "But she doesn't take any trouble to conceal it. And our killer must have an exceptionally devious mind."

"OK. So Alice is above the other two but below the grown-ups. What about Cathy? She seems nice and straightforward but she didn't like Isabella and she's got a crush on Mike."

"Has she?" Graham asked.

"Yes. Definitely. But does that mean she'd kill his wife?" I wondered.

"Possibly." Graham nodded. "I've always understood that jealousy has a strange and powerful effect on the adult mind."

"So ... she had a motive. What about opportunity? Isabella's room was on the top floor. Cathy walked with us the whole way back. I don't see how she could have done it."

"No," said Graham, sighing. "And even if she'd wanted Isabella dead, there's no reason for her to hurt Bruce, let alone Donald."

"But she was there on the cliffs when Bruce died. She wasn't down on the timetable to come along that morning, was she? She said she fancied some fresh air. Could she have done something to the rope?"

"It's theoretically possible," agreed Graham. "But we're still stuck as to the question of motive."

"How about Mike, then?" I asked. "He didn't seem very happy with Isabella."

"But it doesn't follow that he'd kill her," said Graham. "I read recently that forty-five per cent of marriages end in divorce: you'd have thought a legal solution would have been a lot easier than murder. And even if he did want to do away with her, I don't see when he could have done it."

"It's got to link in with the other things," I said. "The deaths that happened before we got here."

Graham's eyes narrowed. "What deaths?"

"Steve Harris – the instructor Bruce replaced. He had a fatal accident in the shower from what I could tell. And the other night I heard Isabella mention the name Richard – he died in South America, I think. Then she started babbling on about ghosts. She seemed to think it was all being done by an avenging spirit or something."

Graham's eyes narrowed sceptically. "Utterly ludicrous!"

"Try telling that to Bruce and Donald. Someone killed them. Or something. It's got to be connected with the past. We've got no choice, Graham. We're going to have to break in to the office."

THE BREAK-IN

WE had a long wait. The afternoon and evening seemed to stretch on for ever, but at last it was bedtime. I waited for Meera and Alice to fall asleep, then I swung myself down from my bunk, slipped on my dressing gown and crept out of the room. Keeping to the edge to avoid creaking, I made my way downstairs.

When I got to the office, Graham was already waiting for me. I tried the door handle. Nothing happened.

"Locked," I said crossly. I didn't have a clue how to get in. "We could go outside and break the window, I suppose." It seemed a bit drastic. Someone was bound to hear. Plus I felt a bit nervous about going outside in the dark, no matter how many times I told myself there was no such thing as ghosts. It looked like my grand plan was going to fall at the first hurdle.

Graham hadn't said a word. All of a sudden he pulled something small out of his dressing-gown pocket and slid it down the side of the door. There was a click; he turned the handle and it swung open.

"How did you do that?" I was dead impressed.

"An old Yale lock is easy to get past if you have the right equipment," he said, holding up a rectangle of plastic. "I never travel anywhere without my library card. It gives you access to a surprising number of places."

We started with the filing cabinets but found nothing that was even remotely interesting.

But when we turned to the shelves my eyes fell on a big brown hardback book with an embossed design on the spine. My mum had something similar at home.

It was Mike's scrapbook.

A load of newspaper cuttings were stuffed between the pages. When I pulled it from the shelf they fell out all over the floor.

The very first one I picked up was about Steve Harris: a short account of his accident. Graham read it over my shoulder.

It seemed that Steve had got stuck in a shower at the gym when the thermostat broke. Boiling water had poured down on him.

"You wouldn't have thought that would kill anyone," I said.

"He'd have suffered third-degree burns," Graham informed me. "If more than a certain proportion of the total body surface is affected – fifty per cent, I think – there's very little anyone can do. And it looks like he was burnt all over."

"Euw!" I winced. "That would be it then. How horrible!"

The next cutting had a bit more information:

Steve Harris was a passionate climber, outdoor sports enthusiast and founder member of his university's expeditionary society. After graduating, he took part in many field trips to remote regions of the world to research the impact of climate change. Two years ago he led a team of friends on an expedition to South America to study the effects of global warming on the glaciers of the Andes. The expedition ended in tragedy when one of the team members, Richard Robertson, died in a climbing accident.

"That must be the Richard Isabella mentioned!" I said. "We've found him."

Graham was already unfolding another bit of newspaper. This one was yellowing at the edges and gave an account of the South American accident.

The group had been climbing above a glacier when a landslide had started.

"'Richard Robertson was fatally struck on the head,'" I read out. "What does that mean exactly?"

"He was killed by a falling rock," replied Graham.

I read the next line, took a sharp, shocked breath and clutched Graham's arm. "Look what it says! I don't believe it! He was roped to Mike! *Our* Mike! *This* Mike! And ... oh my God!" My stomach gave a sickening squeeze. "Mike cut his rope!"

Graham continued reading. "He had to," he said. "Look – it says, 'Climbing conditions had deteriorated so rapidly that the rest of the party were in danger of falling'. Richard was dead already. Mike had no choice but to cut him loose to save the others."

"The others..." I frowned. "Who else was there? What were their names? It doesn't say."

Graham unfolded the next cutting, which had a photograph of the expedition team before they set off. I recognized Mike and Donald. The caption said Steve Harris was the man standing behind them. But what was really odd was the smiling woman at the centre of the photo. Right beside the ill-fated Richard Robertson, her arm tightly around his waist, and smiling up at him with a look of purest devotion, was Isabella.

Things crashed inside my head like a small avalanche. Pacing up and down, I whispered my thoughts aloud, trying them out on Graham as they took shape.

"OK. So maybe Isabella was *Richard's* girlfriend back then…"

"Richard's girlfriend?" Graham said, blinking. "So why did she marry Mike?"

I thought of what had happened to my mum's best friend after her husband had left her. There'd been a whole line of what Mum had called "unsuitable boyfriends". Mum had said, "She's on the rebound. People do strange things when they're unhappy." Had it been like that for Isabella?

"Well…" I said slowly. "Suppose Mike and Isabella were both really miserable after Richard died? Maybe they ended up sort of hanging onto each other for comfort – I don't know. But I reckon Isabella regretted it. They weren't happy, were they? You could see that a mile off. She must have felt guilty. That's why she acted so weird when all this started to happen. That's why she said that she and Mike deserved to be punished."

"Maybe. But you'd have to be certifiably insane to decide to murder everyone. It was an accident, after all. Mike couldn't do anything else."

"Insane…" I said thoughtfully, remembering how Isabella had been on that first night. "You know, I reckon Isabella was a bit unhinged. It's like she was expecting people to die: like she thought they deserved it. She wasn't surprised when Donald fell out of the freezer, was she? And she went back to the house like she was going to her execution. You don't think Isabella might have done it all?"

"How do you mean?" asked Graham.

"Well, suppose she killed the others and then killed herself?" I said.

Graham grunted in response, and considered the matter. "Suicide… It might be a feasible hypothesis," he agreed. "After all, there was no sign of an intruder. And yet if Isabella was behind everything why would she leave Mike still standing?"

"She said she'd had enough up on the mountain. Maybe she tried to kill Mike first and when she didn't succeed she couldn't think up another plan. Perhaps she wanted to die and didn't want to put it off any longer."

Graham looked at the photo, pointing to each of the faces in turn. "Richard Robertson fell just like

Bruce... Steve Harris was burnt... Donald Shaw was frozen... Isabella was poisoned..." His finger came to Mike. "He's the only one in this photo left alive now," he said. "Could he be the killer, do you think?"

We would have carried on talking but at that moment the stairs creaked. Someone was coming! From the heaviness of the tread, I guessed it was an adult rather than a kid and for a second I was gripped by a paralysing, brain-numbing fear. Then the adrenalin kicked in.

Hastily we stuffed the newspaper clippings in the scrapbook, put it back on the shelf and switched off the desk lamp.

"Hide!" I whispered.

"Where?"

There was nowhere to go. The desk was nothing more than a table. There wasn't even an armchair in the room. The only place we could hide was behind the curtains but they were too thin to conceal us properly – we made massive, conspicuous bulges in the fabric, and our feet stuck out at the bottom.

The footfalls stopped outside the office door. The handle moved slightly as a hand touched it.

"We're dead meat!" I gasped.

But whoever was sneaking around in the middle of the night wasn't interested in the office. They had merely paused there for a second, resting their weight on the handle: drawing breath, perhaps, or steeling themselves for something.

After several agonising moments, the soft tread of feet on tiles started again, moving in the direction of the kitchen.

"We need to get back upstairs," I said.

Wordlessly, Graham nodded.

We tiptoed, groping our way across the dark office. Holding our breath, we eased the door open and crept towards the stairs.

We had to go right past the kitchen. Terrified, we saw that Mike was in there, his back to us. The freezer door was wide open and the cold air wreathed about him in misty tendrils. The ice-pop corpse of Isabella was laid on the floor, still wrapped in the duvet. Mike's face was calm as he stroked her hair and said, "It's over now, my sweet. That's what you wanted, isn't it? No more guilt, no more pain. You're at peace now, Isabella. Rest quietly. Sleep for ever."

Mad with grief? Or just plain mad?

Graham and I looked at each other in horror. The icy air from the freezer seemed to drift out into the hall and wrap itself around us when we heard those words. Chilled with fear, we crept noiselessly up the stairs. We parted silently at the top, each of us heading for our own room. But I doubted if either of us would sleep much that night.

For hours thoughts circled inside my head. Mike was the murderer. But how? It wasn't possible. Nobody could have killed Isabella. Nobody could have shut Donald in the freezer. Nobody could have cut that rope.

Nothing made sense. It was too strange. Supernatural. Spooky. Thoughts chased each other round and round, but I couldn't pin down any of them. Eventually I fell into an uneasy sleep, and dreamt about jungles, glaciers and snow-capped mountains.

When I woke up the next morning my head was aching and my eyes felt like they'd been rubbed with hot sand. Blearily I climbed out of bed, grabbed my wash bag and made for the shower.

I stood in the stream of hot water, breathing in the jungle-like steam. Jungles, I thought… Steve. My mind ran through the names of the dead like a teacher calling out the register. Richard Robertson, Steve Harris, Bruce Dundee, Donald Shaw, Isabella Rackenford. Had Mike really killed them all? Was he totally deranged? Because it had to be him, didn't it?

Or could someone else be responsible for everything – someone we hadn't really talked about last night?

Cathy. She wasn't on that trip to South America. There hadn't been anything to link her with the others. So where *had* she come from? Why had she ended up working here on Murrag?

I got out of the shower and dried myself. Cathy had disliked Isabella, I was sure of it – I'd seen the sideways glances she had sent off like poisoned darts at Mike's wife. I was also sure that Cathy liked Mike. But suppose I was wrong? I mean, I'd thought Mike was perfectly sane until I saw him in the kitchen with Isabella's body and then he'd seemed completely demented. Appearances could be misleading. Suppose all those looks Cathy gave Mike weren't loving glances, but something more sinister? Perhaps she'd disguised her real feelings towards him...

Cathy's surname was Price. But could she be related to Richard Robertson and be seeking revenge for his death? If she was his half-sister or his cousin they wouldn't necessarily have the same surname.

Throwing my clothes on quickly, I ran to Graham's bedroom. I badly wanted to talk to him. I opened the door and there was Jake, still asleep and sucking his thumb. Graham was on the top bunk, dozing beneath his duvet.

"Do you think Cathy might be related to Richard Robertson?" I demanded, prodding him awake.

"Erm…" mumbled Graham, rubbing sleep from his eyes. "Maybe…"

My mind was rushing ahead. I didn't know how Cathy could have managed it but… "She was there on the cliffs that first day," I said. "She could have done something with the ropes even if none of us saw it. Swapped them over, maybe, while no one was looking? Yes – that must be it. And then Bruce died by mistake. She must have been furious! So that's the reason for the looks at Mike – she's planning another accident for him!"

"But," objected Graham, "she took us riding the day Donald died."

"Yes. But she went back to fetch her gloves. She was the last person to see him alive…" I trailed off. I'd seen Donald myself when we'd ridden away. I shut my eyes, recalling his silhouette at the window. Realization hit me in a sudden, blinding flash. "That's it!" I squealed. "Suppose it wasn't Donald?"

"In the freezer? But we saw him."

"No! At the window. I saw an outline, that's all – the light was behind him. Someone was there that I *thought* was Donald, but I couldn't see his face. He was standing still. He might have been a cardboard cut-out for all I know. It could have been a trick, don't you see? Cathy could have locked him in the freezer and put the cut-out up. And then when we got back she went straight off to the loo. She could have got rid of it then and none of us would be any the wiser."

"And Isabella? How do you explain that?"

"I don't know. But Cathy was being fantastically cheerful on the mountain, wasn't she? It drove Isabella nuts – that's why she went on ahead of us. I reckon Cathy did it deliberately to wind her up. Maybe Isabella had become so gloomy and doomy that Cathy didn't need to kill her at all. She probably only had to leave the champagne out on the bedside table before we left the house. Isabella would have realized and drunk it to save the murderer the bother."

"There's no proof," said Graham uncertainly.

"No," I agreed. "But I've got a monster hunch that I'm right. I've got to tell Mike! Now, before Cathy adds him to her list of victims."

Leaving Graham in bed, I jumped down the stairs three at a time.

I arrived in the kitchen breathless, still flushed from the shower, with my hair dripping wet. And there, sharpening a knife with immense and scary enthusiasm, was Cathy.

UNDERCURRENTS

I skidded to a halt, hitting my hip on the table with a loud thump.

"Ouch! That must have hurt," said Cathy. "You're up early, Poppy. Why are you rushing about in such a hurry?"

"No particular reason." I forced myself to sound calm. "I was just wondering... Where's Mike?"

Cathy's eyes narrowed. "Mike?" she said, and her voice had a funny edge to it. "He's down in the wood-shed chopping logs for the fire. We'll be needing them if the storm keeps up like this."

I had a vision of an axe embedded in Mike's head in another so-called accident.

"He'll be back in an hour or two," Cathy continued. "Of course, we were supposed to be doing survival skills today, but with Bruce's accident…" She sighed, then attempted a bright smile. It was so forced it looked more like a lunatic's grimace. "I thought I'd take you all for a ride, instead. Are you ready for breakfast?"

"Oh yes," I said. "I'll call the others shall I?" Without waiting for an answer, I turned and fled up the stairs, bumping headlong into Graham as he came out of his room.

"Graham!" I grabbed him by the shoulders. "Keep an eye on Cathy! Make sure she doesn't leave the building."

"How?"

"I don't know! Just keep asking for more toast or something. Whatever happens, make sure she stays indoors."

"OK," said Graham. "Where are you going?"

"The woodshed. I've got to find Mike!" I stopped. Turned. Looked at Graham. "Where *is* the woodshed?"

"It's the stone building at the bottom of the hill," he replied. "But chopping logs is very dangerous, you know. It can cause all kinds of injuries—"

"See you later!" I didn't even stop to put my coat

on. I was off, wet hair flapping across my face, dashing out in my slippers into the wind and rain. I vaguely remembered the woodshed: we'd passed it when we'd gone for that ride along the valley. The lane zigzagged in hairpin bends down to it, covering twice as much distance as was necessary. If I ran along the cliffs a little way, I should be able to find a more direct route – I had to get there as quickly as possible.

I began running, pacing myself so I wouldn't get a stitch or sprain an ankle on the uneven ground. It wasn't long before I came to the U-shaped cleft in the rocks where Bruce had fallen to his death. I paused for a moment to catch my breath. If I turned inland from here, I should be able to scramble down the hill and get to Mike.

The hideous slurping of the hungry sea sent a chill through my veins. It was like a great monster that had swallowed Bruce down. Just like Iain – the man in Bruce's story – both of them were lost for ever.

I started running again, and thoughts banged in my head with each pounding footstep.

A drowned man … a woman who betrayed him … a best friend … cursing their names … never buried … never found … no body ever plucked from the waves.

No body … nobody…

I felt a thought tickling the back of my mind and

had the unnerving sensation that something important was dangling there, just out of reach. If I'd had more time, I would have sat down and worked it out but right then finding Mike seemed like the most urgent thing.

I jogged a little way inland and saw, to my relief, that I was right – there, just a few hundred metres below me, was the woodshed. The trouble was that the ground between here and there was covered in gorse and bracken and densely growing heather. It would take ages to push my way through it. Maybe I could find some sort of track? I scanned the area quickly and noticed a break in the scrub – a faint path – as if someone had made their way down ahead of me.

With my heart in my throat, I began to follow it. But I hadn't gone more than a few metres when something caught my eye.

A large slab of rock was jutting out of the slope, giving shelter from the elements, and underneath it was a long, dry hollow. It was the size of a single bed. Again, I had the tickling sensation that I was missing something important.

I walked towards the rock and saw that the heather beneath it was flattened, as if someone had slept there. To one side was a cut square of grass, as neatly edged as a piece of turf. I peeled it back. Underneath, the earth was blackened and there was a strong smell of ash. A fire had burned there not long ago.

In a blinding flash I realized that the murders had absolutely nothing to do with Cathy! I'd been completely wrong about her.

We'd thought we were alone on Murrag. It had never occurred to me – or any of us – that someone could survive outdoors in the middle of a force-ten gale. But here was solid proof that another person was living on the island. A stranger. No wonder everything had seemed so impossible! Why hadn't I thought of it before?

I was so busy telling myself off for my stupidity that I didn't hear the stealthy gliding tread of an avenging spirit coming up behind me. It was only when a spectral voice uttered my name that I turned.

And came face to face with a ghost.

DEATH SENTENCE

I honestly thought I was going to faint. I went dizzy. My mouth was dry as sandpaper. My legs could hardly hold me up.

It was Bruce Dundee.

Back from the dead. His scarred face dark with fury.

"But you're dead!" My voice was reduced to a tiny, pathetic croak. "I saw you! There was blood in the water. You were unconscious. You got washed away."

"Yes, I did. I'm a ghost. You believe in ghosts, don't you?" Weirdly, all trace of his Australian accent had vanished.

Clutching every scrap of common sense tightly with both hands, I struggled to work out what I was looking at. I fought against the sick feeling that rose in my throat.

Ghosts don't need to make campfires, I told myself sternly. They don't need dry places to sleep. This is not a ghost. It isn't. I stared hard at Bruce Dundee. He looked solid enough.

"OK ... so you didn't die," I said. "You survived that fall. But if you didn't die why didn't you come back to the centre? We were all so upset! Or were you frightened? Was it Mike who cut the rope? Did he try to kill you?"

Bruce Dundee threw back his head and laughed. I felt about a millimetre tall.

Suddenly it was so obvious! My hands went to my head and I dug my fingers into my scalp. How could I have been so thick?

"Hang on..." I glared at him because I knew exactly what had happened. "You did it!" I accused him. "You cut the rope yourself! No wonder we couldn't figure it out."

Bruce didn't answer. Just stood staring at me.

"There aren't any currents around here, are there?" I demanded. "Not ones that suck people down to the depths so their bodies can't be found. You made that story up so we'd think you were dead. But all that blood... What was that? Tomato sauce?"

"Stage blood. Plenty of it. It had to be convincing, you see." His voice was crisp. Clipped. English.

"You knew there was a storm on the way. You knew the coastguard couldn't come so what did you do? Let yourself get washed away and then cling to a rock around the corner? Climb back up once we'd all gone? You're a survival skills expert, so living outdoors would be no trouble at all. I should have worked that out ages ago. And since then you've been hiding out here, picking people off one by one…" I stared at his wrecked face, trying to read his expression. "Why are you doing this? Are you Richard's cousin? Or his friend?"

"I'm not his cousin. Not his friend." Bruce gave a bitter, weird-sounding laugh. "I am him. The man himself. I am Richard Robertson." He did a low, mocking bow.

My jaw dropped. I tried to speak but all that came out was a faint, astonished gasp.

"I suppose you know about the accident in South America?" he continued. "There was an inquest, of course, when they got back. After Mike gave his evidence, Richard Robertson was officially declared dead. I am a ghost, twice over."

"But I don't get it," I said. "Why didn't you get in touch with them? How could you leave your friends like that? Thinking you'd died? Missing you…"

It was like watching a volcanic eruption. Bitterness and hatred poured out like lava. "*Missing* me? *Missing* me? My best friend cut my rope. He left me to die. My pals were so heartbroken they never even bothered to look for me. Do you know what happened, Poppy? Do you want to hear how much I suffered? When I finally recovered consciousness I was at the bottom of a crevasse with a cracked skull, two broken legs and frostbite so bad that I lost half my face to it." He rubbed his hand across his mutilated features. "This wasn't caused by bad plastic surgery after a car crash – this was what *they* did to me! I waited for them to come. But when I'd waited and waited and they still didn't show up I crawled out of that glacier like a worm on my belly, mile after mile down that mountainside. I had to make splints for my own legs. Bandage my own face. When I made it to the base camp, they'd long gone. Do you know what it's like in that part of the world? Of course you don't! I went from snow-capped mountains to tropical forest. From savage cold to unbearable heat. Biting insects. Hornets. Mosquitoes. Snakes. Scorpions. I had to forage for grubs. Insects. Larvae. It took me weeks to reach the nearest village – a few huts in a clearing. No medicine. No painkillers. Hardly any food. It was months before I gained enough strength to get to civilization.

By the time I came home, I'd been declared dead and my best friend had married my fiancée—"

"Mike and Isabella," I said flatly. "So you started to plan your revenge?"

He gave an acid laugh. "What else could I do?"

I looked at him. "The way you killed them – it was all to do with what happened to you, wasn't it? The hot shower that killed Steve Harris – that was like the heat of the jungle. You messed up the thermostat. Wedged the door. Waited. And the same in the freezer that killed Donald – because of your frostbite. You waited until we went out, then you pushed him in. Locked it. Isabella's poison – was that because of the snakes and scorpions?"

He didn't answer directly. "An eye for an eye, a tooth for a tooth… It wasn't revenge. It was justice. Isabella knew that. She let me kill her without a murmur. She was grateful."

The champagne, I thought. The rose petals. Like a wedding. That was sick. "She thought she had it coming. That you were an avenging spirit."

"She always was superstitious," he murmured.

"How did you get out of her room?" I asked. "We were right behind her. Why didn't we see you?"

"I'm a mountaineer, Poppy. I climbed out of the window."

"Of course." It was so obvious! How could we have missed it? I looked at him and said quietly, "That first night... She went so pale when she saw you. I think she almost recognized you."

"But she didn't, did she?" he spat bitterly. "None of them did. My closest friends, and not one of them knew me."

I was starting to get cross. "Isabella felt dreadful about what happened to you, she really did. I heard her! And she regretted marrying Mike. It was all a big mistake. You didn't need to kill her!"

"Oh, but I did. Just as I need to kill Mike. I'm saving him for last. But I want him to lose everyone first, just like I did. I want him to know exactly how it feels to have everything stripped away. But before that, there's the question of how to despatch my dear little cousin Cathy."

"Cathy's your cousin?" I couldn't help feeling pleased that at least I'd guessed that bit right. "But Cathy wasn't in South America! She had nothing to do with the accident."

"No," he said. "But she was at Mike and Isabella's wedding. She agreed to take the job here. She's in love with Mike. Has been for years. That's enough of a betrayal for me." His mouth twisted into a leer. "And now, I'll need to get rid of you too. Mike really shouldn't let interfering little girls wander off on their own. You never know when they might slip, and this cliff-top path is so dangerous. One false step can lead to disaster. So easy to topple over the edge. Another tragic accident…"

I had begun to back away and, as he made a lunge for me, I turned and ran. But my foot caught in a clump of heather and I tripped. Richard Robertson's arms closed around me and a second later I was being hauled towards the edge of the cliff.

DAY OF JUDGEMENT

WHEN something hit Richard Robertson, crashing into him with such force that his legs were knocked from under him, I thought it was an enraged sheep. I hit the ground with a thud and rolled away, spinning beyond his reach. Scrambling to my feet, I started to run. But then I heard a familiar sound, and realized the thing that had launched itself at Richard wasn't an animal at all. It was Graham. And Richard had got hold of him.

Graham's fists were pounding against his captor's arms. "Get off! Get off me! Run, Poppy, run!"

I could see at once that Graham didn't stand any more chance against the lean, wiry climber than I did.

Richard was half lifting, half dragging him towards the cliff edge, just as he'd done with me. They were already perilously close to the edge. Graham's face was white, but still he shouted, "Run, Poppy!"

I had no intention of running anywhere. But if I hurled myself at Richard the way Graham had done, I'd be in danger of knocking all three of us over the edge. Richard had his arms around Graham's waist, and was lifting him off his feet. In a second, he'd launch him into the air, and Graham would plummet into the sea.

As Richard began to swing Graham in a wide arc, I grabbed at Graham's outstretched legs and leaned backwards, hanging on as if it were a lethal tug-of-war contest. But my slippers couldn't get any grip on the wet grass. I tried digging my heels into the turf but I was sliding towards the edge. Richard was too strong. I'd slowed him a fraction, but that was all. With one determined lunge he would throw both of us into oblivion.

A hideous grin, one mad laugh, and Richard swung Graham again. I didn't let go, but I lost my footing, skidded off the muddy grass and started slipping over the cliff edge. Holding on desperately to Graham's legs, I tried to find a foothold. There was nothing below me but air. I looked down and saw the hungry sea reaching up. Above me, Graham – who had been trying to escape Richard's grip – was now clinging to him, frantic to hold on to whatever he could grab. Reaching up, he'd seized a handful of Richard's hair and was clutching it as if our lives depended on it – which of course they did. With a cry of pain, Richard took a step back, then two, three more steps, trying to dislodge Graham's fingers. I crunched hard against the cliff-face and was scraped painfully back on to solid land with each lurching pace Richard took. As soon as I felt the grass beneath me, I let go of Graham and flung myself at Richard's head, tugging at his ears while he lashed out with fists and feet.

We couldn't hold him for long. He'd already prised Graham's fingers from his skull and was bending them backwards with vicious relish. Graham was yelling in agony and there was a horrible cracking sound. I lunged at Richard's nose, but he turned on me and I felt his fist hit me in the mouth. Before we knew it, he had us both by the scruff of the neck like a pair of kittens.

We were done for. This was it. My mouth throbbing with pain, I struggled as hard as I could, hitting and scratching him, but it was useless. The sea crashed on to the rocks below. Any second now we'd both be down there. Claimed by the sea. Lost for ever.

I screamed, hard and high, going on and on without drawing breath until I felt my chest was going to burst.

And then I felt someone's hands ripping us both from Richard's clutches and pushing us back to safety. Mike!

"Bruce...?" he gasped. "What the...?"

"He's not Bruce," I screamed. "He's Richard Robertson!"

Mike looked at me, disbelieving. But then he stared once more into Richard's hate-filled eyes. "Richard? You survived! Oh dear God! Mate, I'm so sorry—"

The noise that came from Richard's throat was barely human. He leapt at Mike and they rolled together, over and over, a tangle of flailing fists, kicking feet and biting teeth. There was nothing we could do but stand and watch, horrified, rigid with shock and fear.

Mike was strong, but Richard was propelled by an anger that gave him superhuman strength. Mike was down. Carried by the speed of his fall halfway over the edge. He was hanging on to tufts of grass, scratching desperately for something to cling to, but they were coming away in his hands. Richard was standing over him. Lifting a booted foot to stamp on his hands.

But then a stone cracked against Richard's skull. He jerked forward. Half turned. Saw Cathy, with her upraised hand. And fell.

*   *   *

I don't want to think about what I saw when we hauled Mike back from the edge. Richard's body was lying, smashed and broken, on the rocks below. As we'd pulled Mike up, the incoming tide had taken Richard again, only this time it was for real.

Graham was nursing a broken finger, I had a loose tooth and a split lip, and Mike's nose was bleeding. But we were alive.

"Where did you come from?" I asked the injured Graham. "I thought I told you to keep an eye on Cathy."

"I couldn't keep eating toast for ever," he replied, looking faintly green. "I had sixteen slices as it was. Sixteen slices! I'm surprised I wasn't sick. She kept sharpening that knife. And then she said she was going off to help Mike. It sounded highly suspicious to me, so I thought I'd better come and find you."

"And how did you get here, Mike?" I asked.

"I was coming back for breakfast," Mike replied. "I heard you screaming."

"It was lucky you came when you did," I said, "or we'd both have been toast."

"More toast? No thanks!" Graham flashed one of his blink-and-you-miss-it grins and then snorted with laughter, and we both sniggered, light-headed with relief, until the sight of Cathy and Mike's serious faces made us pull ourselves together.

We began to hobble back along the cliff path towards the warmth of the centre, Mike breaking it gently to a white-faced Cathy that she'd sent her own cousin toppling over the cliff.

"I didn't know who it was. I didn't want to hurt him," she whimpered miserably. "But he was trying to kill you!"

"The fall finished him," said Graham cheerfully. "Not you. I think they'll call it manslaughter. If we were in America they'd probably say it was justifiable homicide. From a legal perspective I would have thought it extremely unlikely they'd hold you criminally responsible."

"It's not like you woke up this morning and decided to bump off your cousin," I said. "You were defending Mike. It was Richard's own stupid fault that he was so close to the cliff edge. Besides," I added, "he was going to murder you, Cathy. You were next on his list, so don't feel bad. He had it all planned."

"No!" Mike gasped, his face blanching with horror at the thought. "No! Not that!" He shuddered, and slid a protective arm around Cathy's shoulders.

"Why kill me?" asked Cathy, baffled.

"Because you were working here," I told her. "He

thought you'd betrayed him. And ... er ... well, he said you were in love with Mike, and he didn't like that very much."

Cathy flushed deep red, and fixed her eyes on the path. But she didn't push Mike's arm away, and I noticed a look of surprise on Mike's face that turned into a shy, hopeful smile.

There's not much to add, really. Once the storm had blown itself out, the police sent a helicopter over and asked questions about Bruce's climbing accident. They were a bit shocked when they heard about all the murders. Everyone's parents had to fly up to Murrag and there was a whole load of stuff with statements and interviews, but it was pretty dull. Then we were helicoptered off the island, which was as sick-making as the ferry had been but a whole lot quicker.

After all the fuss died down, Cathy and Mike got together and they even opened the centre to proper, paying customers. Graham and I were offered a free week's holiday. They said we'd be guests of honour.

I don't believe in ghosts. Neither does Graham.

But we both turned down the offer, just in case.

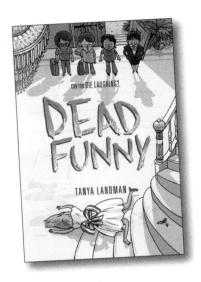

My name is Poppy Fields. I was dead
excited about my first trip to America.
But then people started getting themselves
killed in really weird ways. Nothing made
sense until Graham and I investigated, then
the murders seemed to tie together as neatly
as a string of sausages. A little *too* neatly...

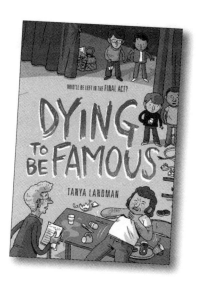

STAGE FRIGHT!

My name is Poppy Fields. When Graham and
I landed parts in a musical, we didn't expect real
drama. But then the star got a death threat and
the bodies started stacking up. Before we knew
it, we were at the top of the murderer's list...

ALSO AVAILABLE:

THE HEAD IS DEAD / CERTAIN DEATH

THE SCENT OF BLOOD / POISON PEN

LOVE HIM TO DEATH / BLOOD HOUND

THE WILL TO LIVE

POPPY FIELDS IS ON THE CASE!